MY HALF DAY

By Doris Fisher and Dani Sneed
Illustrations by Karen Lee

W9-BHG-774

To the Lewis family: Audrey, Philip, Alex, Lauren, and Becky—DF

To my mother and soul mate, Nell Matthews, for her never-ending encouragement—DS

For Tim, my other half—KL

Publisher's Cataloging-In-Publication Data

My half day / by Doris Fisher and Dani Sneed ; illustrations by Karen Lee.

p. : col. ill. ; cm.

Summary: The wacky fun continues as the boy from One Odd day and My Even Day awakens to find a half-head of hair. After chugging down his glass of milk that is two-thirds gooey paste, he and his friend are off to camp for a day of fraction fun and an out-of-this-world soccer game. Includes "For Creative Minds" section.

Interest age level: 004-008.
Interest grade level: P-3.
ISBN: 978-1-934359-14-3 (hardcover)
ISBN: 978-1-934359-29-7 (pbk.)

1. Fractions--Juvenile fiction. 2. Arithmetic--Juvenile fiction. 3. Fractions--Fiction.
4. Arithmetic--Fiction. 5. Stories in rhyme.
I. Sneed, Dani.
II. Lee, Karen (Karen Jones), 1961- III. Title.

PZ7.F57 Myh 2008[E]   2008920385

Printed in China

Sylvan Dell Publishing
976 Houston Northcutt Blvd., Suite 3
Mt. Pleasant, SC 29464

I looked in the mirror.
My hair was a buzz.
ONE-HALF was still long, and
the other **HALF** fuzz!

"Here's breakfast," Dad called.
"There's no time to waste."
My tall glass of milk was
TWO-THIRDS gooey paste!

"The moving van's here with **THREE-FOURTHS** of a ramp. And Donna is waiting. You're riding to camp."

Princess, my dog,
hopped inside the huge van.
We clattered like coconuts
in a trash can.

We stopped at Camp Fraction
and walked through the gates.
FOUR-FIFTHS of the counselors
zipped by us on skates.

We strapped on our quivers for
archery practice,
and noticed the targets were
painted on cactus!

I aimed with my arrow and shut
one eye tight,
then pulled back the bow string
with all of my might.

My bulls-eye was tiny,
ONE-SIXTH of a spot.

No fair!
Donna's was **ONE-HALF**.
She launched the best shot.

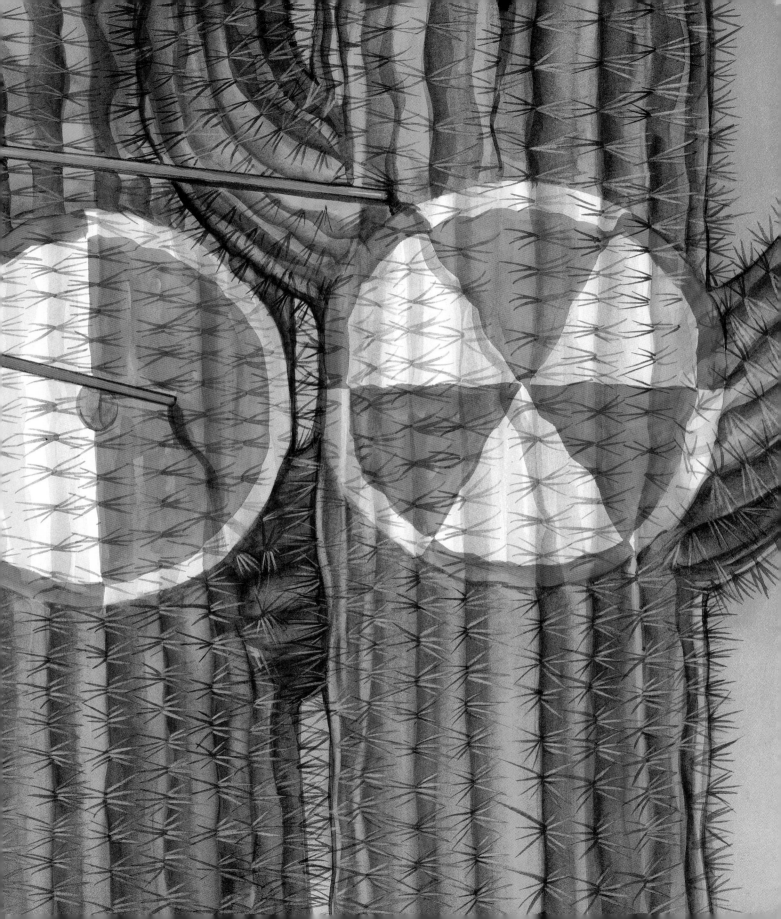

Princess dog-paddled
around our canoe,
when Donna and I
stepped inside as the crew.

HALF FULL

Pink flowers with leaves
floated next to the shore.
We paddled and pulled out
TWO-SEVENTHS of oar!

Miss Dodd is the ref
for our soccer today!
"Each goal counts
FIVE- EIGHTHS," she said.
"Ready to play?"

"The other team's here,
they flew in from the stars."
We stared at the players.
FOUR-NINTHS
were from Mars!

The game was a close one.
Both teams played to win,
but Donna's swift kick
scored a goal with a spin.

The outer-space team
looked both stunned and agog,
as we squeezed 'round a campfire
on **THREE-TENTHS** of log.

We roasted Mars-mallows
and ate Saturn-s'mores.
A rocket ship landed
and opened its doors.

"Climb aboard," said the team.
"Then we'll blast to the moon,
see **TWO-THIRDS** of a comet
and soar back home soon."

Our galaxy trip had
an upside down view.
When we landed on Earth,
I hoped **HALF** day was through.

Then Donna ran home
and I hid in my bed,
with **THREE-FOURTHS** of my
blanket pulled over my head!

Next morning I raced to
the mirror to stare.

Yippee! No more **HALF** buzz,
but a **WHOLE** head of hair.

"Tick Tock," said my Dad.
He gave me a shock.
Today must be **TIME**.
His face is a **CLOCK!**

For Creative Minds

We use fractions all the time

You might break a cookie in **half** to share with a friend.

Football and soccer games are played in **quarters.**

If you sleep for eight hours, you sleep away **one third** of the day.

A **quarter** is worth ¼ or one quarter of the value of a dollar.

Your mom or dad may stop to get gas when the fuel gauge is ¼.

Each time you cut food into smaller pieces, you are cutting it into **fractions**.

Can you think of other common fractions that you use daily?

Measuring and fractions in recipes

One of the most common measures when cooking is "one cup." A recipe might ask for 1 cup of water or flour, but then again, it might ask for ¾ (**.75**) or **1 ½** (**1.5**) cups of flour.

What you need for this activity:
- A complete set of measuring cups
- Raw rice (easier to clean up than flour)
- A large bowl or pot over which to measure to catch "spillage"

Using the rice and the various measuring tools, answer the following questions. Try to guess the answer before "testing" it by pouring the smaller cup amount into a larger cup.

If you use the ¼ (**.25**) cup, how many times would you need to fill it to equal one cup?

If you use the ½ (**.5**) cup, how many times would you need to fill it to equal one cup?

Do you see a pattern?

If you had a ⅓ (**.33**) cup measure, how many times do you think you would have to fill it to equal **1** cup? What about ⅕ (**.20**) cup?

Which measuring cups would you use to measure 1 ½ cups of something?

If you used only **½** cup measuring cups to get the 1 ½ cups, how many times would you fill it?

If you used only the ¼ cup measuring cups to get the **1 ½** cups, how many times would you fill it?

Match the fraction to the picture

Which fraction shows how many muffins are present? 1. _____

What is the fraction missing from the lily pad? 2. _____

What fraction of the cake is strawberry flavored? 3. _____

What fraction of the target is the red side? 4. _____

Which fraction shows how much of the lily pad is present? 5. _____

a. **2/3 or .66**

b. **1/3 or .33**

c. **1/2 or .5**

d. **1/4 or .25**

e. **3/4 or .75**

answers: 1.e, 2.d, 3.b, 4.c, 5.a

1/4   3/5   2/3   7/8   1/4   3/5   2/3   7/

A Pizza Party!

You will need two uncut pizzas. Using a pizza wheel, cut one pizza into eight pieces and cut the other pizza into six pieces.

If you are hungry, would you prefer a slice from the one divided into six (⅙ or **.166**) or eight (⅛ or **.125**)? Why?

Would you prefer two slices of the eight (²⁄₈ = ¼ or **.25**) or one of the six (⅙ or **.166**)? Why?

If you are REALLY hungry, would you prefer four slices of the eight (⁴⁄₈) or three of the six (³⁄₆)? Why or why not? Is there an easier way to say those fractions? What is the decimal equivalent?

EAT AND ENJOY YOUR PIZZA – WHATEVER FRACTION SIZE YOU HAVE!